# *Arthur of the Gododdin*

**Michael A. Ferenz**
**and**
**CJ Brookes**

***Arthur of the Gododdin***

 For information email cjb@litlady.com

FIRST EDITION

Printed in the United States of America

# *Arthur of the Gododdin*

## Table of Contents

**Acknowledgements**

The authors wish to thank Jason Henry for the many hours spent creating the Map of the Gododdin Campaign and Marshall Wren for technical help with publication.

# *Arthur of the Gododdin*

## Introduction

*"My own belief, for what it's worth, is that there was an Arthur, that he was a local war leader, and it all took place in the north of Britain."*

- Professor Charles Thomas
Director of the Institute
of Cornish Studies (2004)

For a thousand years or more, the legend of King Arthur has entertained, intrigued, and inspired audiences of all ages. Authors in the Dark Ages chronicled life in Britain after the departure of the Romans, and suggested a heroic figure brought an extended peace to the land. Nennius, a ninth century Welsh monk, first named this hero – Arthur – and twelve battles in which he was victorious. His sources are thought to be fifth century texts no longer available to modern researchers.

Those lost works and the oral traditions of unknown origins inspired our story *Arthur of the Gododdin*. We asked, as writers do, "what if?" What if Arthur was not a king but a Man of the North, a Gododdin warrior, a warlord? What if there was an old story containing the kernels of truth for all the elements of the Arthurian legend? Read on to discover how we imagine the old story might have been told.

MAF & CJB

# *Arthur of the Gododdin*

## Prologue

*"The key to understanding what sixth-century society in Scotland was like lies in appreciating that the social structure was tribal."*

- Stuart McHardy
*The Quest for Arthur*

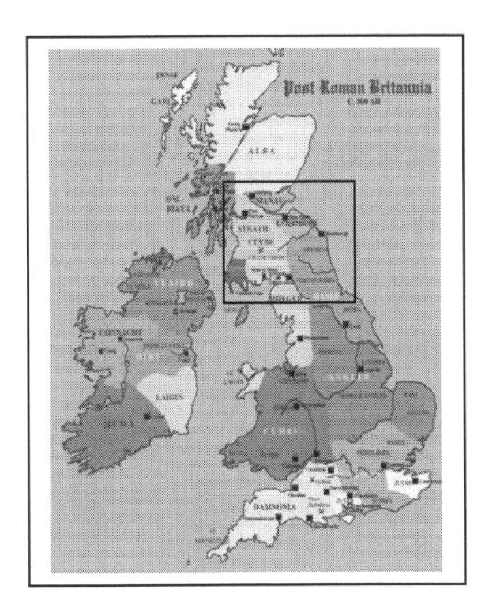


Rheged lies to the north and west on the island of Britain, an area once occupied by the Romans who built their great wall and established Luguvallium (Carlisle) as a town to serve the wall forts. Our small settlement lies nearby on the north side of the River Eden among gently rolling hills and stands of trees lining the water's edge. Our family huts are clustered within an oval enclosure with room for cattle to graze and land to grow crops. A hollow area containing a pond lies at the center. The Gathering Hall faces the gates which are closed at night when the torches are lit.

We are defined by the territory we occupy, and we defend what is ours to the death. All of the men of the settlement are warriors, living by an honor code and only following a leader they respect. Raiding into distant territories and being raided is common practice. Our chieftain chooses the most skillful of the men as battle leader when the need arises to protect our land. Men follow him to gain personal honor.

In days of peace we farm and hunt and fish. The land is green and fertile, the wood is full of small game, and the river overflows with salmon and brown trout. Mother knows which plants and herbs hold the power of healing and when to pick them to ensure the most effective cures. Father prepares the remedies in the wattle and daub outbuilding behind the Hall, grinding the seeds and berries, hanging flowers in bunches to dry under the thatch. As I help them with their daily tasks, the secrets of healing are being passed to me.

Every day in every season I rise with the sun to help with the chores, but tomorrow will be different. It is my eleventh name day, and I am to set out with Father on a great journey.

# *Arthur of the Gododdin*

## Chapter One

*"The secret of the historical Arthur's military successes was his revival of the elite armored Roman/Sarmatian cavalry known as the Cataphracti which had patrolled Britain during the third and fourth centuries. Arthur's adaptation of this highly mobile, highly disciplined cavalry against an enemy that was almost exclusively made up of infantry forces resulted in a military force that rapidly out-manoeuvred, out-flanked, and out-fought its more numerous foes. His twelve undisputed victories against the enemies of his people demonstrated Arthur's ability to command a force of armored cavalrymen to devastating effect."*

- David Day (1995)

North Britain
516 AD

I have had the good fortune to see Arthur on several occasions, and over the years I have come to learn much of my Gododdin cousins. But the first time I did see him, that was a day to remember! I, having seen my eleventh name day, was to accompany my father, a healer, on his summer journey. Each year he made a long journey during the warm months to barter his remedies. This year would be the longest such journey he had ever made, from our home near Carlisle in the west far to the northeast in the land of the Gododdin. We would travel from one full moon to another; Edinburgh would be our final destination.

We left Carlisle, passing through the Wall at old Fort Petriana, following the Roman Road through the lands of the Selgovae, stopping to do business along the way. Our route had made this a passage of learning for me. We passed the tumble-down walls and overgrown cobblestones of the old Roman fort at Burnswark, and further on, our journey turned east at the ruins of another Roman fort called Beattock. Reminded by these sites, Father told me stories of the old Roman times. Father also taught me to gather the roots and leaves needed for his remedies among the oak, birch, and hazel of the Caledon Wood where ran red deer and other wild beasts. The sacred All-Heal, or mistletoe, grew abundant on the oaks, and I gathered much for its calming effects during all illnesses.

At Yarrow, Father showed me the standing stone that marked where two princes of the Selgovae had fallen. He translated the inscription for me. "This is the everlasting memorial. In this place lie the most famous princes Nudus and Dumnogenus. In this tomb lie the two sons of Liberalis." Another stone nearby marked the resting place of other honored warriors who fell in the same battle some seven years ago. This valley was the place where Arthur had led a Gododdin warband to the aide of our cousins, the Selgovae, and the Picts had suffered a terrible defeat. I smiled to know we were following in the footsteps of the great Arthur. Returning home from his travels, Father had oft repeated tales of Arthur's deeds that he had heard in far-flung settlements. The name of Arthur was celebrated.

By now it was May, and the healing herbs were flowering. I gathered many of the pink yarrow rays for Father to use in making his pain-relieving salves. It has long been known that the yarrow or staunchweed was carried with armies to stop bleeding and treat battle wounds, and yarrow tea could clear coryza in a day.

At the Eildon Hills, we entered the lands of the Gododdin and bartered with the villagers there, camping near the old Roman fort known as Trimontium. Father told me, "Here, around the great Eildon Hill North, lives Arthur's tribe. Arthur played here as a boy, and at the age of six had managed to pull the sword from the cairn of stones atop his father's grave only a day after the burial. Choosing the path of the warrior early on, here Arthur learned the way of the war horse. We Britons, as well as the Scots, Picts and Saxons, do not show much skill in the use of the horse in battle, except for the Gododdin."

Pointing to the old earthworks, he said, "Here were stationed Roman Auxiliary cavalry, superb horsemen from a far off place, the land of the Goddess Danu. The Sarmatians they were called, and they lived and fought here with the Gododdin for some 200 years. Their blood runs as one with our cousins, and it is their old way of the warhorse that Arthur, like his great-grandfather Cunedda one hundred years before, has revived. The Cataphracti, the Romans called heavy cavalry, their worth in battle decisive if one knows how to use them. And Arthur does."

A gust of wind hissed through the branches of a nearby tree. Father spoke again. "That hiss is not unlike the sound made by the draconarius of the Sarmatians, the dragon standard that put fear into those who faced it. Arthur now rides with one always near him, as do all the Gododdin warlords. So much so that warlords hereabouts have become known as Dragons."

Days further on, we camped with other pilgrims at St. Mary's Chapel along the Gala Water. We drank from the well there, as Arthur's men had after a hard-fought victory years earlier. "It was here

Arthur called upon the Virgin Mary to guide him in the battle against the encroaching Picts," Father explained to me and several other children in the camp. "He painted her image upon his shield. The chapel where we now camp, Arthur had built in St. Mary's honor." We looked across the valley to the thick pine woods with new eyes, in awe that Arthur had been here. "This dale, this holy field of battle, will always be known with woe."

Father motioned us to follow him into the chapel, and we filed in, greeted by the monk that cared for it. It took a bit for our eyes to become accustomed to the darker interior, but finally we could see her. The Virgin Mary. Her brilliant image painted on a shield that rested upon the altar. We all had to touch it, that shield Arthur had carried into battle, and each of us did so hesitantly as it seemed to radiate a power.

Exiting the chapel, Father said, "Perhaps we will see Gwares. He is one of us from Rheged, and I know his people. Being the second son of a chieftain, he set off years back to learn the warrior's way in Arthur's company."

Finally we arrived at the hill-fort of King Lot of the Gododdin. Passing through the settlement gates at the foot of the huge rock, we were in the shadow of the King's hall, but yet e'en higher there loomed a mighty crag. It was Arthur's Seat, the place where Arthur viewed the ground, formed a plan of battle, and descended with his warband of heavy cavalry to deliver the final victory blow. According to Father, "The Picts were crushed, never again to have power south of the Roman wall named for the emperor Antoninus Pius. This victory made it possible for the Gododdin to re-establish old lands, and for

King Lot to move his hall from Traprain Law here to Edinburgh just two years past."

It was at Traprain Law that King Lot had first set eyes upon Arthur. First as the leader of a warband and later as a warlord of the southern Gododdin, Arthur's fame had spread. Lot often spoke of this young warrior who rode like the Sarmatians of old. Not that many years ago Saxons had put ashore in the southeast and had moved inland to threaten the fortress at Yeavering Bell. The word had gone out, calling for help from Gododdin chieftains. At Roxburgh a force had been assembled, and in it was included the young Arthur and his friends. Mounted they were, and they had drilled and hoped for this opportunity to be part of a warband. Sent ahead to scout as they neared the enemy encamped at the foot of the fortress hill, Arthur seized the opportunity and struck.

Using the concealment of the early morning fog and the woods, the element of surprise, the speed and mobility of his force, and the river and its fording points as allies, Arthur taught the Saxons a bloody lesson in cavalry tactics. First dislodged from their peaceful camp in disarray, then lured into splitting their force and finally in hasty withdrawal, the Saxons, always off guard, were the target of Arthur's many swift attacks. Organized finally, the Saxons abandoned the place of their camp and moved toward the coast. Using the river and its fords, Arthur maneuvered around them. He demonstrated for the first time a coolness in battle that would be his hallmark. Even in the midst of this action, he gauged his time well and ordered all to dismount, water horses, and rest. Appearing now blocking their line of march, Arthur had waited till they were on open ground. Exposed, they were demoralized; several feigned attacks at different quarters exhausted them. In a circling ride, quivers were emptied into them, depleting their ranks. And finally a charge carried home, dropped the Saxons to a man.

"Yes, to a man," Lot always recounted. For when Arthur wheeled his horse around, one Saxon remained. Arthur and his friends rode near to him. He was young like Arthur. Wounded many times, he still stood tall, shield at the guard and sword at the ready. Arthur asked that he surrender, and he refused without hesitation. Some of Arthur's friends made move to finish him, but Arthur motioned them to hold. A moment passed, then Arthur moved to throw a skin of water to the Saxon. "Sheath your sword and sling your shield; go home," said Arthur. Later he told his friends that it is good that one survives to tell the story.

The late morn was spent scouring the battlefield. Helms, armor, shields, swords they all had now. The next time they fought they would truly be heavy cavalry. And as they moved, the elation of victory never overcame them, yet they were in awe of what they had done. The battle had gone by so quickly that they had not time then to think of its events. They had all fought hard, but they knew the victory belonged to the many commands Arthur had given. Arthur had led from the front. Now they were Arthur's warband. In honor of this victory, Lot ordered a battle stone mark the spot along the River Glen in the shadow of the Bell.

The King had summoned Arthur to Traprain Law to make judgment upon his worth, and so satisfied, then deemed him Warlord of all Gododdin. There, too, Arthur met for the first time, his mother's sister. Vivian had left the southern Gododdin when Arthur was just a babe to become one of an order of priestesses. The King had requested her presence at the ceremony that would make Arthur the Pen-dragon and that she bring the sacred sword that was in safe keeping with her order. The people were in much peril with enemies threatening from all points, and Arthur would need, and should carry, a sword of destiny. The Sisters of Mother Earth saw in those words great merit, and so they came to Traprain Law from the Isle of May, Vivian carrying the sword Caliburn. Forged from metal that had fallen from the heavens in a time ancient before the Druids, this sword, said to have been carried by Andrasta herself, was placed in the hands of Arthur, defender of his people. With it, a bronze scabbard crafted for Arthur displaying the old ogham marks declaring his immortality in battle. This scabbard had itself helped to fulfill the prophesy it proclaimed. Swinging wildly in battle, it had been at the right place at the right time, blocking many an enemy blow and protecting Arthur's left as Bedwyr did Arthur's right.

## Chapter Two

*"There is a palace of Arthur the Soldier, in Britain, in the land of the Picts, built with various and wondrous art, in which the deeds of all his acts and wars are seen to be sculpted."*

- Lambert de St. Omer (1120)

And now at Edinburgh the hope that I had nurtured during our journey was dashed. Arthur had departed the King's hall just this morn with his hundred heavy cavalry, on his way back to his frontier fort at Camelon. I had hoped upon hope that I would have a chance to see Arthur, this fierce Gododdin warlord whose name is spoken by the enemies of Britain in only a whisper.

Camelon! The old Roman Legion city just north of the Antonine Wall and south of the River Carron that Father had mentioned often. With the departure of first the Imperial Army to Rome and then the Gododdin warlord Cunedda's army to aide our threatened cousins in Wales, the Picts had over-run the region called the Manu-Gododdin. Camelon was a key in control of the Manu, and so when Edinburgh was secure, Arthur marched the Gododdin army there, driving the Picts out in a great battle. The Picts rallied north of the River Carron, assembling a great army themselves at the ancient Bassas. They attacked across the river near where the old Roman Road crossed it. The recapture of Camelon their goal, a terrible defeat is all that they gained. Camelon would become Arthur's fort/city/home and, for a time, the River Carron, the frontier between Pict and Gododdin.

That eve Father and I were busy tending to many with common ailments at the King's settlement, and that night all slept well. But the morning was a flurry of activity. A rider had come in at cock's crow.

Arthur called all Gododdin warriors to make haste to his side. Returning to Camelon, Arthur had happened upon a huge Saxon force that had beached forty hulls at the mouth of the River Avon. It was said one thousand barbarian warriors were ashore on Gododdin land. Arthur had engaged them at first, but with only his one hundred heavy cavalry, the enemy shield wall could not be turned or broken. Arthur had withdrawn to the fort atop Bouden Hill, sending riders to Camelon and Edinburgh for aid.

By late in the day a relief column had been organized and formed. The King's Warband of two hundred spears and fifty cavalry was to march to Arthur led by Gawain, the King's eldest son. King Lot bade the warriors the speed of a white hart and that they make a hearty feast for the ravens. Next to the King stood his new bride Anna, the sister of Arthur, holding a babe. She held little Medraut high so the gathering of warriors could see him. She said, "This is what you fight for, the children of the Gododdin, the future of your people." At that moment, Medraut thrust a little clenched fist into the air. All the throng roared with a cheer, and Gawain bellowed, "It is a sign of victory." Then the King's Warband was off, the column moving down through the settlement, out the gate, and to the west. They were gone.

Days passed with no word. Worry hung heavy on all. Yes, Arthur had given the Gododdin eleven great victories these past years. But if the message had been correct, the numbers were heavy on the side of the Saxons. One thousand Saxons. Arthur had his hundred heavy cavalry, and Gawain had marched out with two hundred infantry and fifty cavalry. The odds did not bode well, and no word made all uneasy. If Cai could reach Arthur as well, the battle would go better. Many prayed that Cai, who could field a warband similar to Gawain's force, would be at Camelon when Arthur's word arrived there, and that he was not away on the frontier engaged with the Picts.

The turbulent frontier is now the River Forth and the Ochil hills. After Camelon, Arthur had projected the power of the Gododdin army further north to retake all that had been the Manu. Around the River Forth and Stirling, he had fought a victorious campaign of four battles. The first secured the Stirling hill fort on the south of the River Forth. Then across the Forth and using the old Roman fort on the north bank as a base, he struck the Picts up the Allen Water valley. Next, moving east along the Forth, a battle was fought at Clackmannan. Finally the Picts struck back, marching around Dumyat and down toward Stirling. Arthur met them on a flat-topped hill above the valley floor. Defeated once more, the Pictish army began a withdrawal, this time with Arthur in pursuit. Fearing the loss of part of the Ochil Hills to include sacred Dumyat, the Pict king sued for peace, and even offered a daughter in marriage "when she comes of age." Eager for peace after four defeats and with respect for Arthur the Warrior, the Pict king made this serious offer. For with the Picts, a matrilineal line of succession is observed, thus Arthur could someday be a Pictish king himself.

After the first of these four battles, Arthur noted a round earthwork that sat below the Stirling hill fort. He chose a night to have the army assembled around by torchlight, and he mounted this table of earth. He called up from every warband, men who had distinguished themselves in battle to receive praise from him and the army. Revered warriors such as Brychan, the nephew of King Lot, Blaes, Cadog, Aron, Cyon, and Gwares were celebrated, their heroic deeds sung.

Gwares, for one, was a hero at the battle at the River Carron. In the midst of the fiercest fighting, Arthur's dragon standard had fallen, its bearer cut from his saddle. In a wild frenzy, the Picts seized it up; a trophy of victory, they thought. Gwares charged in, his warhorse and he as one, a giant wild boar flashing a deadly blade. Arthur's dragon standard must not fall to the enemy, and amidst swirling horsemanship and singing steel, the Picts fell from the standard one by one. Gwares took it up and rode to Arthur, taking a position just to the rear and left of him. Bedwyr looked to his left. The dragon standard held in Gwares left hand snapped in the wind, and a blade dripped red in his right. A huge grin spread across Bedwyr's face from cheek plate to cheek plate. Arthur glanced back over his left shoulder, and, with a nod to Gwares, clicked the hilt of Caliburn to his helm. After the battle, Arthur would not take the standard that Gwares offered back to him, but bade him carry it at his side always.

Arthur, atop the round table, then spoke of some of the great warriors that had died in battle. He asked that all in the army think of one they knew that had fallen a hero. He drew Caliburn. "Pull your swords," he said as he did his, and a field of blades now bristled around him. Holding Caliburn high, Arthur spoke, "Let us not forget those who have gone before us. Let our actions be worthy of their deeds and sacrifice in the defense of our people.

> *"We are more than just warbands, we are more than an army, we are more than soldiers, and we are more than lords. We are all a brotherhood of warriors; we are the Gododdin."*

Arthur then repeated this ceremony on several nights of the following week as more warbands of the Gododdin arrived to swell the ranks of the army for the push across the River Forth and the three battles that would retake the Manu.

A last battle fought in the Manu was at the Fords of Frew and against an invasion force from a western Pict kingdom. After four hard-fought battles in succession, Arthur's army responded yet again by marching west along the south bank of the River Forth. His leadership inspired them, but they were tired. Arthur again allowed a portion of the Picts to cross the Fords and then struck, knowing that he could defeat that number. But could he then force a crossing himself, to fight the larger part of the Pict army on the northern bank? If so ordered, Arthur's men would not hesitate to do so, but it would be a huge risk. As the Gododdin finished off the Picts across the ford and secured it, another large force appeared from a woodline north of the River Forth and to the west. The Pict army would be huge now, Arthur thought, larger than any he had ever faced. A fighting withdrawal to the safety of Stirling so his men could rest and be reinforced might be wise. But what of the people? The Picts would be to the south of the River Forth and raid deep into Gododdin territory. Arthur shifted uneasy in the saddle. Then a cheer seemed to be sweeping thought the Gododdin ranks, and Gabhran, second son of Domangart, rode up to Arthur.

"Scots. They are Scots, my people of Dalriada," said Gabhran, pointing at that force coming from the woodline. Arthur rose in his saddle to watch. The Scots, enemy of the Picts for over a hundred years, now swept forward in a wild headlong charge. Arthur noted that he had never seen infantry move at such a speed. As their blood-chilling war cries echoed across the valley, they crashed into the flank of the Picts. Arthur watched. It was not a battle of shield walls but rather a hornet's nest of wild warriors who lived for the moment. In the midst of it all, small areas cleared, and the battle paused as champions from Scot and Pict squared off for single combat. In the end, the Scots flank attack was too much for the Picts. After defeat and heavy losses, these Picts withdrew to their hill forts up the River Teith valley.

So it was that Arthur met the commander of the Scots, Gabhran's brother Comgall ap Domangart, King of the Scots. That night the two great warlords shared food, stories, and the warmth of the campfire. A mutual respect and bond was formed between them, friends they would be.

## Chapter Three

*"The twelfth battle took place at Mount Badon,*
*at which a single assault from Arthur killed 960 men*
*and no other took part in this massacre."*

- Nennius (circa 800)

It was late afternoon and three days had passed since Gawain had marched out. A young boy of my age rode hard to the settlement. He had ventured west that morn to scout. Like an arrow, he shot through the gate and up the long way to the King's hill-fort. King Lot stood upon the top step of his hall as the boy reined up and thrust his fist holding two javelins into the air. "Victory! Arthur has won a great victory. The Saxons are all dead!" Arthur's column would arrive well before the sun fades. This boy had ridden with the column for a time and was told the story of the battle, a story retold a hundred times e'en before Arthur arrived.

The Saxons had moved inland along the River Avon and had besieged Arthur and his cavalry atop Bouden Hill. There Arthur waited for three days until messengers from Gawain and, thank God, Cai came to Arthur. Gawain with the King's Warband held to the east, and Cai with the Manu did so to the west. The messengers wondered why they were not sent at once to give the attack order. But Arthur had a plan; he always had a plan. The dispatch of the messengers was delayed some hours, and Arthur's horsemen used this time to ready themselves, then they were sent back to Cai and Gawain. These two forces of infantry supported by cavalry now moved up to show themselves to the Saxons. Activity below showed there was some concern among the invaders. These two small forces of foot soldiers on the east and west of the river, were they vanguards of larger forces? Arthur hoped that was upon the Saxon chieftain's mind. The Saxons blinked first and began the move down river to some safety near their boats and away from Bouden Hill. One force of Saxons moved toward the ford to cross and move to their boats along the west of the River Avon. The other half of the Saxons force moved north along the east bank, making good time, toward their boats. Their army was split. Arthur smiled.

Cai's infantry allowed some to cross the ford and then moved in to form a shield wall stopping their advance and blocking their path. The battle was on. Cai's infantry blocking the ford fought hard, but surely they would give, being outnumbered so, or did they fight in this manner because they knew something? Horns sounded back near the hill, and all turned to look. Arthur had led his heavy cavalry down from Bouden and had formed in a long line in the flat at the hill's base, facing the back of the Saxon force crossing the ford. Shields, helms, and spear points glittered in the sun, and ribbons tied to each spear danced in the wind. Arthur's spear dropped to point at the Saxons. The war horns sounded once more. Arthur's cavalry was on the move. From a walk to a gallop in a flash, the charge would take the Saxons head on. A cheer went up from Cai's infantry.

The ground thundered as the Saxons not yet across the ford tried to organize themselves, but fear now gripped them, for few had ever faced cavalry in battle, and those that had, knew how gruesome could be the outcome. Arthur was upon them, and the ill-organized Saxon line met the charge, but it could not stand. Spears shattered, and Saxons were thrown back and trampled. It was akin to a run away cart rolling into a field of barley only to stop when its momentum was spent after doing so much damage. Cai now put in a charge with his fifty cavalry into the flank of those across the ford. That was it, the Saxons were broken and ran in panic, each one trying to survive.

Arthur now rode out of the melee to open ground where the charge had started. He sat on his horse now facing north along the east bank of the River Avon. Soon Bedwyr joined him as did his hornsman and standard bearer. Recall sounded, and Arthur's heavy cavalry re-formed in another long line.

Cai's infantry were making short work of the few Saxons that had survived the ford battle, and his cavalry with their horsebows were hunting down those scattered and trying to escape. The larger half of the Saxon army moved for their boats north along the east bank of the river. Gawain's infantry rushed in to form a shield wall, anchoring its right flank on the river, and with its left protected by Gawain himself and his cavalry. The Saxons charged and let loose their throwing axes. Gawain's men braced themselves as the Saxon axes rattled off their shields, and then the two shield walls met with a crash. The terrible close-in fighting of infantry was on.

Unable to flank the King's Gododdin because of Gawain and his cavalry, the crush of Saxons slowly pushed back Gawain's infantry line. Then they echoed again, Arthur's war horns. All heads snapped to look on the heavy cavalry advancing at a walk. Most of the spears of Arthur's cavalry had been broken in the fight for the ford, so this battle would be fought with sword and shield. It was like lightning, the flash above the Gododdin heavy cavalry, as swords were drawn and held high. The Saxons formed a second shield wall to meet the cavalry charge, their two walls now standing back to back. Gawain's infantry fought hard to stand their ground, but were giving some way. The Saxon shield wall prepared to meet Arthur's charge. It was tight, compact and steady. Arthur's cavalry approached now at a trot and then veered to their right and away from the Saxons. Cheer upon cheer roared from the rear Saxon shield wall. They had held fast. They had turned Arthur's cavalry. Those cheers were answered by even louder ones from the front shield wall of the Saxons as Gawain's infantry gave way and swung back from the river. It was akin to a beaver's dam giving way and the whole mass of Saxons surged forward toward the Firth and the safety of their boats. Close to the beach now, the Saxons topped the last roll of land and looked down at their boats. Terror struck them as the moving mass came to a halt, and a sickening groan spread through their ranks. They looked upon their boats, all sitting at an awkward tilt upon wet ground. The tide had gone out. No escape.

Could the Gododdin now exploit their own terrible plight? Gawain's force was spent having carried out such a hard-fought, delaying action, and Cai's was far off at the ford. Could Arthur's cavalry somehow reform after having broken off their attack? Could they strike now at this moment of truth?

The day could belong to the Gododdin, if, only if… Then, cheer upon cheer went up from Gawain's force as through the dust of what had been their infantry battle, Arthur's cavalry emerged at the full gallop and swept past them. One moment forced to break off a charge, and the next reformed and descending on its prey like an eagle. It was Arthur's Warband at its best.

Arthur in the forefront with shield held at high guard and Caliburn pointing at the foe, Bedwyr at his side. The Gododdin's feared dragon standard hissed in the wind, and war horns sounded eerily, echoing above the thunder of horses. This charge would be carried home into the ill-prepared mass of demoralized Saxons. They had dared to invade the lands of the Gododdin, the lands of the great warlord Arthur. No quarter would be given. At the beach Arthur's Warband was like a scythe in autumn, the foe cut from standing. They lay in bundles still upon the ground. The victory was decisive and complete. Later that day the Gododdin army rested in long shadows as their fallen brothers were wrapped in their cloaks and put to ground. Arthur would miss them, but he knew someday that they would all sit together in the Hall of Shields with Cunedda, Boudicca, and Caratacus.

Worry hung heavy upon Arthur as the sun set that Galahad was not accounted for. Galahad, a lion in battle always, yet the devout goodness of his soul was what he lived by. He had arrived at King Lot's hall not long after Arthur, and they had become friends at once. A warrior of some note, he had taken the sword of a Saxon prince in battle. When the King called for one to seek out his daughter and return with her, Galahad accepted the quest. A journey of danger it would be, taking him deep into Pictish country. The King's daughter Thenew had had a falling out with Lot some years before and had fled in a small boat out into the Firth. It was thought that she had perished. This did trouble the King, but he learned that she had made the other shore and was granted refuge by one known as St. Serf. Galahad, with his friends Peredur and Bors, had succeeded in this adventure, and Thenew was well received in the King's hall. With her she brought a gift for the Gododdin, a chalice that St. Serf had acquired upon pilgrimage to the Holy Lands.

Thenew, having observed Galahad and making note that he must be deemed a good man by God every day, asked the King that he be proclaimed Guardian of the Chalice. The King received this request well and answered by also naming Galahad his champion. The seat of the King's champion was a perilous one. Previous champions had fallen in battle not long after being chosen, but Galahad had managed to survive several battles, though having been wounded in each. Many said it was the Holy Chalice of which he was guardian that protected him.

Now into the glow of Arthur's campfire came Bors and Peredur leading their horses and a third, atop which sat Galahad. Wounded again he was, but would recover once more. Arthur sighed with relief and rose to greet them.

At the ford and at the beach the ravens made a wild feast.

## Chapter Four

*"Bedwyr son of Rhyddlaw*
*With nine hundred listening*
*And six hundred attacking*
*Was well worth watching"*

- "Par Gur,"
*The Black Book of Carmarthen*
*(circa 1250)*

The King and Queen welcomed the exhausted army home, and that late afternoon and eve were spent tending to the horses, arms and armor, and the wounded. The King declared that tomorrow would be a day of remembrance, victory and salvation, and all understood that first the warriors must address the needs of their craft.

I assisted Father long into the night, tending to the many wounds of our Gododdin cousins. The moon was past high when Queen Anna stopped to thank Father for his efforts. The Queen's apron was soiled, and I knew she had been working as we had. I was in a bit of a daze when I realized the Queen was speaking to me.

"My child, you are exhausted," she said and led me to a bench, fetching up a bucket of water and a cloth on the way. "Sit here with me," she said, and I took my ease next to her. "You have worked harder than your father, I should think, but you must always take some time for yourself," Queen Anna said as she washed my face and hands.

Eiddilig, lying near by, a bandage round his head, rose up on one elbow to say, "That little one did see to my cut and to the needs of many others here. A special touch she has, my Queen."

"Well, you are celebrated among Arthur's warriors," Anna said, finishing cleaning my face.

I managed to say, "Thank you, Queen Anna."

"Oh, it is I, on behalf of the Gododdin, who owe you thanks," Anna said, slipping a pendant from around her neck and over my head. I looked at it, a beautiful bronze horse it was. "It is a symbol of our Gododdin culture. All will know you are one of us," Anna said. A huge smile came to my lips as I clutched the horse to me. "And it is a symbol of the Goddess Epona, should you choose to follow the old ways, but that is for you to decide some day," the Queen said.

I ran to Father to show him the horse, and, of course, he had been watching the whole time. We looked back to the Queen. She rose from the bench with a smile and a nod, gone from the fire light she was.

Of the battle I did learn more later that eve'n from Arthur's closest friend Bedwyr who stopped to warm himself at the fire that my father and I shared with many from the King's settlement. Bedwyr, making his way to the King's hall, after an inspection of the horses, now sat among us, rubbing his hands near the fire.

A boy spoke, "Tell us of the day of battle, Bedwyr."

He answered, "Ah, I am tired and you will hear it all told tomorrow, but I will tell you this." And Bedwyr began.

*Atop Bouden Hill, besieged for three days, vengeful rage overcame Arthur. How dare these barbarian pirates make shore upon the land of his people? When battle came, he proclaimed, "Be merciless." No quarter would be given.*

*At the ford, Arthur's Cavalry was the dragon and he its fiery breath, for he led the charge in the van, the first to strike at the foe. This was as always and why he was renowned,* Bedwyr explained to his rapt audience. *The greatest respect of his men he is honored with. We will follow no other.*

*Arthur was just off my shield arm and his steed's length ahead. As his spear point dropped, war horns sounded, we went straight into the gallop. The charge was on. The draconarious banner hissed next to me. The Saxons tried to form their shield wall, but it was hurried and not solid. There were gaps, and Arthur made for one. Over the shield wall, I caught a glimpse of the Saxons who had crossed the ford against Cai's Manu Gododdin shield wall. The terrible push and crush of close-in fighting on foot, slaughter at its peak. Almost on them, the faces of the Saxons said all. Terror, it was Arthur! Arthur's war horse at full gallop struck the foe's loose line. Its scaled armor rattled as Saxon shields and spears shattered. Arthur, with skill not known to many, danced his spear tip from Saxon helm to helm. They fell limp to ground, their necks snapped. On his left arm his shield moved like a darting swallow. A throwing axe glanced off and another. An ashen shaft shattered against it as its edge moved to cleave foe's face. Several rushed at Arthur's right, and I rode in, my spear drove deep into one and was pulled from my grip. I went to my axe and cleaved the others. The force of such a blow from horseback cuts clean through helm, shoulder, and shield. The charge at a stop now, our horses were whirlwinds in the water of the ford, trampling upon man, arms and armor.*

*Arthur looked to his left and in a flash let his ashen shaft fly. A Saxon almost pulling one of his Warband from the saddle took the point square in the back. As if one movement, Arthur pulled his three javelins from their sleeve, two to his shield hand and one at the ready while sidestepping his steed to bowl over yet more foe under hoove. A Saxon in brilliant armor, a chieftain, emerged from the fray to Arthur's right and raised a gold-hilted sword to strike. He moved his arm forward but only his shoulder responded, his arm and sword cleaved, my axe thrown. Now Arthur's hollywood flew, one – two – three javelins, each striking the back of a Saxon facing Cai's line. A Saxon leapt from the mass, bare hands gripping the top of Arthur's shield. Arthur struggled to stay in the saddle. Then a gray flash, and the Saxon was no more. Cabal, Arthur's mighty wolf-hound, had struck, carrying his prey by the neck to ground.*

*Cai and his horsemen now charged what organized Saxon force was left across the ford and took them in the flank. The work of his heavy cavalry completed at the ford, Arthur rose in the saddle to give Cai a salute, and a roar went up from Cai's Manu as they saw him.*

*Arthur reined his steed around and rode from the dying melee to a place near where the charge had begun. This time he faced the Firth and the other half of the Saxon army that had moved toward their boats. For a moment, he stood there alone, the image of a war god. I moved to his right side once more, and soon his Warband reformed. Arthur knew they would be with him even without a horn sounding the recall. Arthur knows his men, each a titan in battle.*

Explaining to us again, *To refuse retreat earns the reward of heaven and a man is worth nothing without might and courage. We all know the words – 'Everyone dies when Fate so decrees.' Arthur would ask so much of us now, a second charge, a second battle. I looked at Arthur, at my good friend's face, and I saw confidence. My horse stepped side to side and front and back, as did all the war horses. They were up to it.*

*In the distance, the clash of battle could be heard. Gawain and the King's Warband were blocking the Saxon advance to their boats. All looked to Arthur, and it seemed that the day fell silent; the air pinched at my skin. Then it happened. Arthur's right hand moved across his body, grasped its hilt, and Caliburn, the ancient leaf-shaped blade that spelled dread for the enemy, cleared its scabbard with a ring and was held high. His Warband followed and a bright blue flash broke over the heads of his cavalry line, like a breaker crashing ashore on the Isle of May.*

*Arthur pointed Caliburn forward, and with the sound of a horn, the line stepped off as one, not at a gallop but at a walk, and though we moved now slowly, all war horns echoed, discordant and ominous. Shields were raised and the hilts of swords struck the back of them rhythmically, the sound of thunder. The Saxons against Gawain heard it, then saw us. The rolling wrath of a terrible storm was coming, Arthur's Cavalry, war horns, thundering shields, and now war cries.*

*The Saxons formed a second shield wall to face us back to back with the one that pushed Gawain's infantry. This one was solid, shields overlapped. Spears bristled many ranks deep. Arthur increased the pace to a canter, and the foe braced. It would be a terrible clash. But then, Caliburn was leveled and pointed to the right, and his Warband responded as we had many times upon the parade ground. As we veered from the shield wall, the Saxons went wild, cheering and letting war cries loose. They had turned Arthur's attack.*

*Arthur now sat in the midst of a giant pinwheel of cavalry and all looked to the dragon standard just behind him to mark their place in the maneuver. Gawain, whose cavalry with horsebow and javelin was keeping the Saxons from a flanking of his shield wall, now saw the moment. Arthur's host was halfway through making a circle, Gawain spurred his steed to his infantry. It was time. He ordered them back in a wheel away from the River Avon. With a cheer, the Saxons surged forward toward the Firth, their rear wall, elated with having stemmed Arthur's charge, turned to follow. "To the boats, to the boats," went the shout. I looked at Arthur, calm he was, his shield held low at his left and Caliburn resting upon his scaled armor at the shoulder. At the canter the whole time we had been, and full circle we had come, and as we came to face where the Saxon line had been, the line reformed on the move and we now stalked them as they made their way to the Firth.*

*My horse, as well as all, was now hard to control, almost wild. The horses knew the day was not over. Arthur moved to the fore, his shield came up and his sword flashed high to come pointing at the foe. The most bitter and cruel war cry I have ever heard him utter came from his lips. War cries swept up and down our line. The horns sounded the loudest of the day, and we sprang as one to the charge. Moving now like a dragon at its prey, we swept forward. The Avon on our left, horses vaulting Saxons, a feast for ravens made by Gawain's brave infantry. On our right now, Gawain's shield wall sent up cheer after cheer as we thundered by, and Gawain flashed his sword in a salute. Ahead, the Saxon mass stopped as their lead topped the last low rise before the shore. Disorganized, they froze. Elated they had been just minutes before, and now dejected they stood. The tide was out, their boats of no use, no escape. Good luck for the Gododdin, you might say, yet the delay in sending the messengers back to Gawain and Cai had a planned purpose. Arthur knew when the tide would be out and timed it well. Arthur is as much in touch with Mother Earth as he is with horsemanship.*

*The loose mass spun to look at us, too late to form up. The dragon struck. Arthur, just ahead of me, let out war cry upon war cry, his steed moving at a speed I have not known. The hem of his red cloak snapped just over my shield, flowing straight out behind him like wings. It was held at his right shoulder by a brilliant fibula in the shape of a cross, given to him by Anna just days before on his departure from Edinburgh. This day an avenging angel he was. His horse struck the first foe with a crash of doom, and the Saxon flew to pieces. His horse driving into foe after foe, their bodies hurled back and into others, Caliburn cleaved down those to his right swinging in great circles, and my horse rode down those who escaped its wrath.*

*I rode in Arthur's wake. A long boat running ahead of a storm, he was – cutting a swath of slaughter through a sea of Saxons. And the spray of Arthur's wake covered me. It was red. In the time of a hoot, ten Saxons Arthur had laid low, and there was near one hundred of us. My Lord did not stop till he made the line of high tide ebb, and I was with him all the way. With Arthur, I turned my wild steed to look back, my blue blade dripping red. There was hardly a Saxon standing, the field before us a harvest of Odin's sons. Gawain's cavalry swept in and took down the survivors of our charge with horse bow and javelin. A few foe, throwing off all armor, made the water's edge and swam to one boat far out and afloat. Arthur looked at them and said, as he often has, "It is good a few escape to tell the story. All the Saxon tribes will hear that the land of the Gododdin is a place of death for them."*

*The victory cry carried from Arthur to all his Warband.*

Bedwyr paused for a moment, looking into the embers of the fire and nodding his head slightly. We had hung upon his every word. "That was a day to remember," Bedwyr said.

The boy among us spoke again. "How many of our enemy did you slay, Bedwyr?"

Standing now in the campfire light, the perfect image of a warrior, Bedwyr bellowed, "I laid low fifty Saxons."

As Bedwyr turned to depart the fire, the boy snapped to standing and said,

"Swift, steadfast a bull
Hosts are dread before you
Your blade is death
Bedwyr, most renown of the Gododdin."

His departing now checked, Bedwyr turned to us. "Yes, true that is, though I am no Arthur.

## Chapter Five

*"Behind Arthur came his cavalrymen, rank on rank, carrying shields marked with images both savage and sacred, with point and blade spears. Some carried bows and javelins or long lances. Some wore iron helmets and wild animal skins. Others wore linen combined with plate armour or mail. Some wielded axes taken from the Saxons; still others proudly brandished their heavy Roman cavalry swords.*

- David Day (1995)

But now to the moment I had been waiting for all this trip. Father and I, our cousins, all lined the Royal Mile that wound its way from the settlement gate to the King's hall atop the rock. Twelve victories he had given his people in these past few years. The air was magic in anticipation of his coming. The cheering that had started down near the gate grew closer and closer, yet I could not see Arthur mounted and high above the crowd. Suddenly foot soldiers were passing us, the men of Manu and of the King's caer marching as one. I turned to Father. "Where is Arthur? Should not he lead the army?" I asked.

A man next to us replied, "Arthur thinks too much of his infantry to make them march in the dust of the cavalry. The shield wall sets the battle that allows his heavy cavalry to win the day. Arthur will lead the massed horsemen at the end of the army."

I cheered the infantry. Tall and round shields of white passing me by for some time. Now a gap in the parade, and I noticed that some even eased back a bit from the edge of the route. What is this?

Padding along was the savage wolf-hound Cabal, his stalking glance sweeping side to side. "Cabal!" I shouted, and not thinking much of it, I rushed out. Cabal stopped to look at me with a bit of a start, and the crowd near gasped. I threw my arms around his neck in a huge hug and gave him a kiss. "Cabal, are you well?" I asked.

"And a hero's welcome for Cabal as well. Not many dare, and he allows even fewer to approach him." I looked up, and it was Arthur speaking to me with a smile. "You have a gift, child," he then said. Arthur, Bedwyr, Cai, and Gawain riding four abreast reined up for that moment, and my father hugged me back into the crowd, Cabal giving me a lick on the cheek and a li'l yelp before moving on.

And now the moment I had hoped for, Arthur was passing me by, his steed's scaled bronze armor jingling. I looked up. A silver helm he wore, crowned with a gold dragon and gold plates dangling at his cheeks. At his neck, a thick torque of gold and a collar of amber. His blood-red cloak flowing, held at the shoulder with a gold cross fibula. Scale armor of gold and white enamel hugged his torso. Caliburn swung at his side. His shield of white wood with a bronze edge and boss bounced lightly upon his horse's flank. It bore the Virgin Mary's image and glittered with its many rivets of silver and gold. Trews of a wide band, blue and white crossing pattern, set him in a leather four-horned saddle. His right hand held a dark shaft spear, topped with a silver-leafed point, the bright of it even in the daylight like a star. And then he was gone. Arthur, I thought, and I had seen him.

Then, not far along, the cavalry was called to a halt. I rushed ahead between horsemen and crowd to just past Gawain. An old warrior lay in the road, and those near were helping him to his feet. Standing with the aid of a wood slat, he had been cheering Arthur's approach, sword in hand, and had slipped, falling into the parade's path. Arthur handed his spear to Bedwyr and swung from his saddle, as did Cai and Gawain. Arthur walked to the old one, now helped to standing, glancing at the sword now upon the ground.

"I cry your pardon, Arthur. My legs do not hold me so well these days."

Arthur extended a hand to his shoulder, saying, "Are you well, brother?"

"Aye, aye," said the old warrior.

Arthur looked to the sword at their feet. "I would look upon your blade, should you allow it," he said.

"Of course, of course, though it is not much now," was the reply.

"And you must look at mine as well," said Arthur as he drew Caliburn and held it high, its bright blue blade shining like lightening. My gaze was fixed upon it as was the look of all nearby. Cai knelt to take up the old sword, and Arthur handed Caliburn to his brother warrior. The old one was beaming as he looked upon Caliburn, the thumb of his hand holding the hilt, rubbing the red stones inlaid in the crossguard, and the fingers of his other hand gently moving along the blue blade. Arthur examined the old blade he received from Cai. A spartha it was with a simple riveted wood hilt not as long as it had once been, the tip severed and refashioned. Arthur spoke, "This blade has seen much service. It has stung many a foe and been ear to many a soldier's talk around the campaign fire."

"This blade is the savior of our people," the warrior said of Caliburn.

"In honor of your service, at tomorrow's victory feast you shall sit at the end of the bench," Arthur said, turning to Gawain.

"I shall see to it, Arthur," Gawain replied.

"Next to me, we shall drink wine from glass," Bedwyr bellowed from the saddle.

Swords returned and a salute of brothers exchanged, Arthur, Cai, and Gawain moved to remount. The old warrior returned to the crowd, renewed life running through him, those near wanting to touch the sword that Arthur had held.

I ran. I ran up the road toward the King's hall till I had no breath, and found a place near it to watch. I must see Arthur one more time, I must. And here came the four horsemen once more. High above Arthur, the bronze dragon-head of his standard with its red sock body floating a horse length behind. A cool wind welcomed Arthur to his people, and the marsh reeds in the dragon's mouth hissed victory. Resplendent and gliding along amidst a hero's welcome, I saw in Arthur all that was strong and kind, courageous and just, generous and honorable of we Britons. Leonides, Caesar, Hannibal, and Boudicca all in one, the warrior hero for all times – Arthur.

## Chapter Six

*"Who is there, I ask, who does not speak of Arthur the Briton, since he is less little known to peoples of Asia than to the Britons as we are informed by pilgrims who return from Eastern lands? The peoples of the East speak of him as do the West, though separated by the breadth of the whole earth. Egypt speaks of him, nor is the Bosporous silent. Rome, queen of cities, sings his deeds, and his wars are known to her former rival Carthage. Antioch, Armenia and Palestine celebrate his feats."*

- Alain de Lille (1170)

The first time I saw Arthur – that day on the Dun Eiden rock – has lived in my memory and my heart for all the days since. Now as an old woman, I sit by the hearth fire and tell all who would hear the story of the day I first saw Arthur. That day lives in my heart as it does in the memories of the men who set aside their weapons after that victory. For indeed, peace came to the land of the Gododdin after the battle of Bouden Hill.

Not to say there weren't skirmishes on the borders and challenges to Arthur's companions, but Arthur's reputation spread and his deeds were told to the ends of the known world. Bards carried his story, each telling the tale in his own way. As a fili of the north, I, too, am a teller in the bardic tradition, but remember, I was there. I mayhap tell the stories differently than you have heard them before for these are the tales of Arthur from his homeland in the north where the children are raised on stories of their kinsman Arthur. His deeds echo among them like the hiss of the draconarius over the charge. Arthur is a byword for valor among them. Wherever the Gododdin do battle, they bring ravens to feast for Arthur forever rides with them.

## Epilogue

*"The grave of March, the grave of Gwythur,*
*The grave of Gwgawn Gleddyvrudd;*
*A mystery to the world, the grave of Arthur."*

- "The Verses of the Warrior's Graves"
*The Black Book of Carmarthen*
*(circa 1250)*

There are many other stories I can tell of Arthur.

Remember the Pictish king that sued for peace with Arthur?

And that daughter he promised to Arthur when she was of age? Two years after Bouden Hill, Arthur waited at Camelon. Much anticipation and excitement gripped the settlement and fort. Of age now, the daughter promised in marriage to Arthur by the Pictish King Ogrfan was to arrive. Arthur was vexed with taking a woman that he did not know as his bride. But this marriage would form an alliance that the Gododdin needed. With threats to the east and south, it would secure the northern frontier. The first of May dawned pink with promise as Guinevere rode through the main gate of Arthur's fortress. Making her way to Arthur's hall, she was cheered and gifted with flowers the whole way. They met as Arthur helped her from the saddle, he noting her beauty and she his presence. Love at first sight, I should think it was, and the people were so very happy for them. In the days to come, Arthur learned of Guinevere's kindness to all, her common sense and logical approach, and her great wisdom. She became Arthur's most valued counsel. Guinevere found in Arthur courage against all odds, honor-bound devotion to his men, and unflinching duty to his people. When not in battle, Arthur was at his best when she was with him, and

Guinevere beamed at his side. They were scarcely apart those many years, until that fateful day that they kissed each other farewell, and Arthur mounted his warhorse for the last time to do battle at Camlann.

Mordred, what a fine young man he grew to be.

King Lot passing on when Mordred was young, he looked to Arthur as a father. Becoming a warrior and horseman, he was a loyal and fearsome addition to Arthur's company. Anna worried so at him being away on campaign, but she knew that Arthur would look out for him. Mordred did marry Gwenhwyfach who was Guinevere's older sister. Another union of alliance but love never sparked between them; perhaps it was the age difference. With the death of Ogrfan, Mordred was in fact a Pictish king, but spent little time with Gwenhwyfach at his fort of Barry Hill. Rather he wished to be with Arthur's warband. A Pictish king, yes, but Gododdin warrior prince suited him better. Mordred would learn of Gwenhwyfach's dealings with the Saxons and her scheme to retake the Manu with a Pict/Saxon army. With knowledge of this betrayal and escaping from confinement ordered by Gwenhwyfach, Mordred set out on a perilous journey to warn Arthur at Camelon. Arriving just a day in advance of the Picts and Saxons, there was time enough for Arthur to prepare an evacuation to Edinburgh. But this column of civilians would move slowly, and Arthur knew he would have to buy them some time. Mordred refused to go with the column to Edinburgh and took his place in the ranks of Arthur's warband as it rode out to meet the Pict/Saxon army in battle.

Few would survive that bloody battle of Camlann which halted the enemy advance. Arthur, though old, would not die easy and fought to the end defending the dragon standard. At Arthur's side a valorous warrior fell with him. He was called Mordred.

In the twenty years that followed the Battle of Bouden Hill, the Gododdin enjoyed a relative "time of peace." Not to say that Arthur did not lead his army upon campaign in those years, but it was nothing like the yearly combat of his campaign of twelve battles. In that time of peace, Arthur extended the arm of Gododdin army beyond its territory. To speak of some …

The southern frontier became alive with continued Angle incursions into Gododdin territory. The Cheviot Hills south of Trimontium became a landscape of constant raids.

Arthur mounted a campaign to clear these raiders out and to strike at their base along the River Rede. It was a massed Gododdin army that Arthur led south that spring: the men of the Manu, the King's men of Edinburgh, warriors of the Bell, and Arthur's people of the Eildon Hills. All the chieftains and warlords of the Gododdin rode with Arthur, and in a day-long turmoil of battle, the Angles were broken and put to flight from High Rochester.

Arthur went on campaign to repay the Scots for their assistance at the battle of the Fords of Frew. He marched west from Camelon, encamping near Glasgow and Dumbarton. There his Strathclyde cousins joined with him to march north, and, along with the Scots, fought battles against the Picts at the head of Long Loch and Loch Lomond. These devastating defeats near Ben Arthur gave those of Strathclyde and Dalriada years of respite from continued combat with the Picts.

To Rheged Arthur came with his army to thwart an advance by the Angles. Their purpose was to establish a foothold in the Bewcastle Fells along the Liddle Water with final intent to cut off Rheged from its cousins in the north. Arthur positioned his army near the hill that today bears his name, Arthur's Seat, and the men of Rheged anchored their army at Carby Hill. These cousin armies sent the Angles packing after a savage battle, the Angles not to venture again into that district for fifty years to come thereafter.

The "time of peace" was also a time of diplomacy for Arthur. He traveled to have counsel with the Selgovae, the Dumnonii, and the

Novantae. Excursions took him to Dalriada and Rheged, voyages to Wales and Brittany. Guinevere loved to be with Arthur on these journeys, and Arthur always sought her advice in talks with the leaders of these peoples and lands.

The trip to Brittany was Guinevere's favorite, quite an adventure it was. There was extensive preparation for the many ships required. Arthur was to purchase many a mount there. His cousins of Brittany were known for their breeding of quality horseflesh, and Arthur needed to replenish the herd of Gododdin warhorses. The King of Brittany drove a hard bargain, but it was all worth it in the end.

Guinevere was as much the center of attention as Arthur. The Bretons had never seen one of the wild and savage Pict race whose women are even known to be warriors.

Guinevere did disappoint in that she was not an amazon, but won all over with her charm, beauty, and wisdom. She would say, "Born a Pict, yes, but my heart is Briton, Gododdin."

In the year 537, the scribes recorded,

> *"The Battle of Camlann in which Arthur and Mordred fell; and there was a plague in Britain and Ireland."*

Mordred had arrived at Camelon only a day in advance of the Pict/Saxon army. The fort and settlement were empty now, except for Arthur's company of horse warriors. An evacuation organized in short order, the column of its civilians now moved toward the safety of Edinburgh with Arthur's infantry to guard it. The northern frontier had been peaceful the past twenty years, and Camelon had become a comfortable place for Arthur and his warband to grow old. The young Gododdin warriors now did seek glory in the south where the frontier with Angles was alive with conflict. Gwenhwyfach's treachery was complete, for there were no warning signs that the Picts would break the peace. Brychan's position at Stirling had been compromised with the Saxon's landing on the south of the River Forth. He evacuated the people of the Manu west toward Dalriada and safety with the Scots while sending what horse warriors he had to Arthur at Camelon.

Arthur would not be able to set this battle with his infantry. The speed and shock value of his cavalry would have to win the day. Arthur would meet the enemy on open ground across the ford and north of the woods that covered the crooked glen on the River Carron.

It was a crisp late morning with a good breeze off the Firth that Arthur deployed his cavalry in line from the woodline. Arthur and his warband stood there looking at the foe, the only movement being the pennants that flew from each spear point. They were resplendent, each man wearing all the finery accumulated over twenty-five years of victories. There was no doom or foreboding among them. Few with silver hair have a last chance at glory, to die with sword in hand. They did not fear the enemy. They did not fear death, for they knew they would all meet again in the Hall of Shields. A last charge. The grip on spear and reins tightened, and the horses clawed the earth. Then a shaft of sunlight broke through the overcast and illuminated the Gododdin horse warriors. All looked up to see a flight of ravens circling, and a groan could be heard from the enemy ranks, as, one by one, they landed upon the helms of the Gododdin, the last lighting upon Arthur's helm.

The ravens sat there looking at the Gododdin foe, and Bedwyr bellowed, "Victory! Once more we ride with Arthur to victory!" The ravens took flight at the Picts and Saxons, and Arthur's spearpoint dropped to point at the enemy battle line. The Gododdin war horns sung a death knell for the enemy, and Arthur's cavalry was on the move, the last charge that would seal their place in immortality.

Arthur's battle plan had served the Gododdin well that day. The mobility and striking power of his cavalry, he had maximized to its full potential. In that first glorious charge, Arthur had employed several maneuvers that confused the enemy. He and Bedwyr, each commanding half the cavalry, had breached the enemy line and slaughtered the Pict and Saxon warlords along with their band of bodyguards. It was a good way to start the battle, the two headed serpent void of leadership. The enemy line transformed into small groups of men that rallied around lesser leaders, those chieftains more concerned with a 360 degree defense than advance upon the ford. After hours of charge and counter-charge, the enemy was in disarray, a patchwork of small bands withdrawing to make the safety of Stirling by nightfall. Arthur, with only a handful of his company, the horses and riders all but spent, sat looking out over a battlefield of chaos. Even then, an ad hoc band of Pict and Saxon showed some purpose in moving toward the ford. In that last charge to protect the ford, and in the furious melee that ensued, Arthur and his men fought like mother bears protecting their cubs. Arthur finally took a spearpoint and fell from the saddle. Lying there, he saw Mordred circling him, hewing down the enemy in his defense. But in time, under Saxon axe and sword, Mordred fell next to him. Arthur knew the end was near and gripped tight the hilt of Caliburn.

With the thunder of horses, Arthur thought he had drifted off to dream. But no, it was Bedwyr, charging in with the last few warriors he still had mounted, to finish off the Picts and Saxons near Arthur. Arthur told his old friend to make his escape, and Bedwyr just smiled. With a few mounted and a few on foot, Bedwyr organized a party to carry Arthur from the battlefield. Moving along the shore of the Firth, they came across a beached boat, and with it, Vivian and others of her order. Arthur and those badly wounded were put aboard. Arthur and Bedwyr smiled as they finished some talk and clasped hands. They knew in the end they would meet again and sit together in the great hall, its walls covered by the shields of the host of warriors within, and they would await the final call to arms. The boat cast off in the fading light, bound for the safety of the Isle of May. Bedwyr drew his sword, holding it in salute, he called out over the water,

"Leader, warrior, brother kinsman
Red stained spearpoint attacking
Death sung by blue blade
Swift before the charge
Most worthy to lead
Foe-men in terror flee
Graves for foe-men that stand
No quarter given
No retreat made
Bear in the turmoil of combat
Slayer of enemy hosts
Celebrated, loved, renown champion
Dragon of the army
Arthur, Gododdin king of battle."

Sailing away, Vivian stood and held Caliburn high in a salute to Bedwyr and the few that stood on the shore, asked to do so by Arthur who could not manage it. Bedwyr looked across the water to Caliburn glowing in the sunset. “It is a sign of victory,” Bedwyr said. “Arthur will return to us when we are in danger, to again lead a charge to victory.”

# ***Theory***

# ***&***

# ***Support***

## Our Theory

### Introduction

For we Arthurians, Arthur represents a hero for all times. Valor, loyalty, honor, compassion, he exemplifies to us. When you strip away the literary and mythical Arthur, you find he is even more extraordinary, a titan in his historical setting, Dark Age Britain. It is a testimony to Arthur that those who admire him seldom say, "I would have liked to have been Arthur," rather they say, "I would have liked to follow Arthur."

In arriving at our theory of a historical Arthur, we have studied the primary pre-Galfridian sources as so many have before us. Those being Gildas, Nennius, the *Annales Cambriae*, and *Y Gododdin*. Regarding each of these sources, volumes have been written offering numerous and varying interpretations on the identity of the authors, the time and place the works were composed, and the time and place to which they refer. To that, add the many avenues of research that have explored Arthur's connection to each. Then mix in the lay of the land, linguistics, religion, tribal customs and the warrior's way of the time. And there you are at the beginning of a journey in the search for Arthur, with a daunting number of paths and detours to that end.

### Theory

So many have gone before us, and we have cherished every minute spent reading their works. For what it's worth, here is what we think. Arthur was a sixth century Gododdin warlord leading a band of heavy cavalry in a campaign to secure the lands of his people.

**Support**

"The Northern Arthur theory," according to Thomas Green in *The Monstrous Regiment of Arthurs* (2004, p 3) "is one of the most respectable theories of a historical Arthur…This model takes its concept of a historical Arthur from chapter 56 of the *Historia Brittonum* – that is, it sees him as a late fifth-/early sixth-century warrior famed for leading the fight against the invading Anglo-Saxons. It then uses the nature and perceived regional bias of the very earliest stratum of Arthurian sources to argue that these sources imply that this Arthur was originally a hero of *Y Godledd*, the 'Old North' (that is northern England and southern Scotland)…"

Norma Lorre Goodrich claimed to "offer the first historical proof of the existence of King Arthur" in 1986 (p.3) Yet John Morris in 1973, detailed *The Age of Arthur*, and reminded readers that WF Skene wrote of the historical Arthur a century before (p. 457). Northern Theory proponents such as Alistair Moffat reason that "historians have failed to show convincingly that King Arthur existed, for a good reason: they have been looking in the wrong place..." (1999, flyleaf) His theory places Arthur in the north of Britain, lowland Scotland today. Others support this premise from their own perspectives as professional researchers, amateur historians, scholars of oral traditions, and Arthurian enthusiasts. Storyteller and folklorist, Stuart McHardy's *Quest for Arthur* explores the tribal culture of sixth century Britain. "Strip away the romantic trappings of chivalry and idealised feudal kingship and even chivalry can be seen to echo the honour code of the tribal warrior – an honour code that respected the individual above all and in which no man could follow another he did not respect." (2001, p 2) J.E. Russell's paper sheds light on the possibility that Arthur fought more than twelve battles, and "suggests sites for twenty-three battles fought by the historical Arthur in Scotland." (2005, p 2)

Arthur, sixth century war leader (*dux bellorum*), forged a reputation recognized across the known world. To quote a twelfth-century commentator on Geoffrey of Monmouth's *Prophetiae Merlini*, Alain de Lille (1170), well-respected French theologian and poet, "Who is there, I ask, who does not speak of Arthur the Briton, since he is less little known to peoples of Asia than to the Britons as we are informed by pilgrims who return from Eastern lands? The peoples of the East speak of him as do the West, though separated by the breadth of the whole earth. Egypt speaks of him, nor is the Bosporous silent. Rome, queen of cities, sings his deeds, and his wars are known to her former rival Carthage. Antioch, Armenia and Palestine celebrate his feats." (Alanus de Insulis c. 1170). At a time when one victory could lead to renown, Arthur became known for twelve victories. Nennius, eighth century historian, apparently had access to no longer available fifth century sources and recorded battles at sites no longer found on maps in an order more recognizable as a bardic list than an historical campaign. "The twelfth battle took place at Mount Badon, at which a single assault from Arthur killed 960 men and no other took part in this massacre." (cited in *Medieval Sourcebook, p 9/Camelot Project p 3*).

"The secret of the historical Arthur's military successes was his revival of the elite armored Roman/Sarmatian cavalry known as the Cataphracti which had patrolled Britain during the third and fourth centuries. Arthur's adaptation of this highly mobile, highly disciplined cavalry against an enemy that was almost exclusively made up of infantry forces resulted in a military force that rapidly out-manoeuvred, out-flanked, and out-fought its more numerous foes. His twelve undisputed victories against the enemies of his people demonstrated Arthur's ability to command a force of armored cavalrymen to devastating effect." So says David Day, (1985, p 18) poet and author, who goes on to say, "Behind Arthur came his cavalrymen, rank on rank, carrying shields marked with images both savage and sacred, with point and blade spears. Some carried bows and javelins or long lances. Some wore iron helmets and wild animal skins. Others wore linen combined with plate armour or mail. Some wielded axes taken from the Saxons; still others proudly brandished their heavy Roman cavalry swords." (Day, 1985, p 18) His revival of and innovative genius in the use of cavalry against enemy foot soldiers, led to victory after victory, and respect from followers, kings, and even his enemies.

He lived and was remembered for three generations before legend "engulfed his memory." (Morris, 1973, p xiii) According to Lambert de St. Omer, Benedictine chronicler and abbot lauded for his great learning, "There is a palace of Arthur the Soldier, in Britain, in the land of the Picts, built with various and wondrous art, in which the deeds of all his acts and wars are seen to be sculpted." (St. Omer, 1120) Several discoveries in the twentieth century suggest we might be just one discovery away from finding the real Arthur. For example, Troy, the legendary city of the *Illiad* and the *Odyssey*, was only first discovered and excavated in the 1930s. It took until 1977 for archeologists to discover the three royal Macedonian tombs at Vergina dating back to the time of Alexander the Great. The legendary Camelot of Arthur and his burial site on the Isle of Avalon have not been discovered, yet. As recently as 2003, a chamber grave reminiscent of the Sutton Hoo ship burial site was unearthed during a survey for road improvements in Essex. Under the verge between the road and the railway line, the chamber grave of a seventh century East Saxon king lay intact as sand had filtered into all the spaces and supported the roof timbers, keeping the grave frozen in place since about 630 AD. Why couldn't there be a "palace of Arthur" waiting to be discovered "in the land of the Picts"? Even Professor Charles Thomas, archeologist at Tintagel and Director of the Institute of Cornish Studies in 2004, commented in Francis Pryor's 2004 DVD *King Arthur's Britain*, "My own belief, for what it's worth, is that there was an Arthur, that he was a local war leader, and it all took place in the north of Britain."

Currently housed at the National Library in Wales, the *Black Book of Carmarthen* is a manuscript dating to the middle of the thirteenth century. It is believed to have been the work of a single scribe at the Priory of St. John in Carmarthen. Much of the material either concerns figures of the Dark Ages or are religious poems. For instance, in the "Par Gur" Bedwyr is described as "Bedwyr son of Rhyddlaw, With nine hundred listening, And six hundred attacking, Was well worth watching." (Evans, 1906) In "The Verses of the Warrior's Graves," (Evans, 1906) the tomb of Arthur is mentioned as unknown even then.

"The grave of March, the grave of Gwythur,
The grave of Gwgawn Gleddyvrudd;
A mystery to the world, the grave of Arthur."

## Four Primary Sources

### Gildas

Gildas, a sixth-century monk, is regarded by some as the "earliest British historian,"[1] since his *De Excidio Britanniae* "is almost the only surviving source written by a near-contemporary of British events in the fifth and sixth centuries."[2] By his own description in Chapter 26 of *De Excidio,* he supports the date of the siege of Badon Hill, "when took place also the last almost, though not the least slaughter of our cruel foes, which was (as I am sure) forty-four years and one month after the landing of the Saxons, and also the time of my own nativity."[3] *The Catholic Encyclopedia* dates his birth to "about 516, in Scotland on the banks of the Clyde (possibly at Dumbarton), of a noble British family."[4] As a contemporary of Arthur living the north, it may seem strange that Gildas does not mention Arthur in his writings. His silence has been explained by Caradoc of Llancarfan (circa 1155) and Gerald of Wales (1188) as revenge for the death of Gildas's brother at the hands of Arthur.[5] Richard White comments that Gildas himself asserts "that the British rulers do not deserve to hand their names down to posterity."[6] A more literal interpretation suggests that the criticisms he leveled against the kings of Britain do not include Arthur because he was not a king.

White also interprets the "siege of Badon" as "(probably modern Bath)"[7] Robert Vermaat writing in *Vortigern Studies* concluded, "Gildas may well have been moving about during his life, even during the time in which he compiled his work. The later traditions all refer to Gildas' leaving Britain, both to Brittany and

Ireland. Nevertheless, if one would speak at all of a location that seemed better equipped than another, or one in which Gildas spent more time if you like, I would certainly opt for the south-west, and particularly for the Durotrigan region."[8] That is, modern Dorset, south Wiltshire and south Somerset, placing Gildas in the region of Bath, Glastonbury, and Cadbury Hill, yet he does not identify any of these locations with Mt. Badon or Arthur as later researchers have done.

In Gildas we have a northern-born, near-contemporary to Arthur who makes reference to the date of the battle of Mt. Badon but does not give locations or names, other than Ambrosius Aurelianus, perhaps because these pieces of information would be commonly known to his readers and not needed to support the purpose of *De Excidio Britannia,* which was a criticism of the kings and priests of Britain, and not intended to be a history, as we understand that term.

**Gildas Notes**

[1]Edmonds, C. (1909). St. Gildas. In The Catholic Encyclopedia. New York: Robert Appleton Company. http://www.newadvent.org/cathen/06557c.htm . Retrieved April 22, 2009 from New Advent.

[2]Gildas. From Wikipedia, the free encyclopedia. http://en.wikipedia.org/wiki/Gildas. Retrieved April 22, 2009.

[3] Gildas. *Concerning the Ruin of Britain* (De Excidio Britanniae). Medieval Sourcebook. http://www.fordham.edu/halsall/source/gildas.html Retrieved May 18, 2011.

[4] Edmonds, C. (1909). St. Gildas. In The Catholic Encyclopedia. New York: Robert Appleton Company. http://www.newadvent.org/cathen/06557c.htm . Retrieved May 18, 2011 from New Advent.

[5] Caradoc of Llancarfan, *The Life of St. Gildas* in *Arthur of Britain*, ed. Sir E.K. Chambers (London: Sidgwick & Jackson, 1927) pp262-4, trans. R.D. White

[6]White, R (ed.) (1997). *King Arthur in Legend and History*. London: J.M. Dent. P 21
[7]ibid P 3
[8] Vermaat, R. "Where did Gildas Write?" Retrieved April 22, 2009. http://www.vortigernstudies.org.uk/artsou/gildwhere.htm.

**Nennius**

The *Historia Brittonum,* History of the Britons, is attributed to an eighth century Welsh monk by the name of Nennius. In the seventy-six chapters of the text, he traces the history of Britain from its Celtic and Roman origins to the Anglo-Saxon period[1] in a chronological and geographical manner, interspersing descriptive stories and genealogies of known persons.

From the end of Chapter 50 through Chapter 55, Nennius discusses the life and work of St. Patrick primarily in Ireland. Having turned his attention to the north in this part of the text, he lists in Chapter 56, the battles of Arthur, the dux bellorum, and the kings of Britain against the Saxons, followed by, in Chapter 57, the genealogy of the kings of Bernicia who reigned in the area once known as the land of the Gododdin or, as the Romans called them, the Votadini, the Men of the North. This area we know today as Northumberland in England and East Lothian in Scotland. By placing the list of Arthur's twelve battles in this section of his work, the chronological/ geographical organizational pattern Nennius used in the *Historia* points to locating these battles in the north.

Since Nennius's locations are not to be found on today's maps, the list does remain open to interpretation. Arthurian scholars have used Nennius's list to locate the battle sites from southern England to Wales, from Lincoln to Carlisle, but there is one point of consensus among researchers. "The seventh battle was in the forest of Celidon, that is Cat Coit Celidon."[2] Translated from the Old Welsh, this is the Battle of the Forest of Caledonia. This ancient forest covered most of the area of Selkirkshire and Dumfries and along the upper Clyde and

Tweed rivers, in Caledonia, the old name for Scotland. If Arthur fought a campaign of twelve battles against the Saxons that included a battle in the Celidon Woods of the north, it seems reasonable to locate the other eleven battles in the surrounding area in the north. The twelfth battle in which Arthur was victorious was on Mount Badon, a battle mentioned by Gildas, Bede, and in the *Annales Cambriae*, which can also be interpreted to have taken place in a northern locale.

## Nennius Notes

[1]Nennius. From Wikipedia, the free encyclopedia. http://en.wikipedia.org/wiki/Nennius Retrieved April 26, 2009.

[2]Nennius. *Historia Brittonum*. Medieval Sourcebook. http://www.fordham.edu/halsall/basis/nennius-full.html . Retrieved April 26, 2009.

***Annales Cambriae***

According to *The Annals of Wales*, these events occurred in the following years.

- 516 The Battle of Badon, in which Arthur carried the Cross of our Lord Jesus Christ for three days and three nights on his shield and the Britons were the victors.

and

- 537 The Strife of Camlann, in which Arthur and Medraut perished; and there was plague in Britain and Ireland.[1]

Arthurians cite these two passages in support of the historicity of Arthur and the dates of the battles. Since all other persons mentioned in the *Annals* are known to be historical figures, it stands to reason that Arthur and Medraut also lived. In addition to dating the Battle of Badon, also mentioned by Gildas and Nennius, the *Annals* connect Arthur's final battle at Camlann with the plague in Britain and Ireland. This time of great death in Britain and Ireland has been compared by M.G.L. Baillie to a "dust-veil blot[ting] out a lot of sunlight, presumably around the whole northern hemisphere"[2] Using information from ice-core samples, tree-ring studies, and volcanic eruptions, he concluded "there can be no doubt that some momentous happening took place in the mid-sixth century AD"[3] that he calls "the 536-45 event"[4] which resulted in "famine, death, and population disruption."[5] Given that the first mention of the Battle of Camlann occurs in the *Annales Cambriae* and modern scholarship supports the date of 537, "it is safe to say that the only plausible written source for the date of the battle of Camlann is the *AC* [*Annales Cambriae*]"[6]

## *Annales Cambriae* Notes

[1] *The Annales Cambriae. Medieval Sourcebook.* http://www.fordham.edu/halsall/source/annalescambriae.html. Retrieved April 27, 2009.

[2] Baillie, M.G.L. (1995). *A Slice Through Time: Dendrochronology and Precision Dating.* London: Routledge. P 93.

[3] ibid

[4] ibid

[5] ibid

[6] Wiseman, H. (2002). "The derivation of the date of the Arthurian entries in the *Annales Cambriae* from Bede and Gildas." Vortigern Studies http://www.vortigernstudies.org.uk/artgue/guesthoward.htm . Retrieved April 27, 2009.

***Y Gododdin***

*Y Gododdin*, the elegiac poem composed sometime before the year 638 by Aneirin, records the march of the Men of the North, the Gododdin, against the Saxons and their subsequent fall at the battle of Catterick. Scholars consider the poem to be "of vast cultural importance,"[1] since it is "the earliest known major work of literature in a native language of the British Isles,"[2] Old or Early Medieval Welsh. "The *Y Gododdin* is considered by many historians to be one of the most convincing pieces of evidence in favor of a historical Arthur, due to its early date, clearly historical conception of Arthur, and historically plausible content overall."[3]

The poem describes the tribal society and warrior life of the Old North. In its stanzas readers find warriors whose "courage and fierceness in war" contrast with "generosity and liberality in peace."[4] The themes of loyalty, hospitality, fate, and heroism expressed through metaphors and symbolism[5] are consistent with the heroic ideal: sadness at the loss but celebration of the courage in earning undying fame.[6]

The heroes of *Y Gododdin* are compared to famous heroes not of the warband, "paragons of excellence and prowess, for emulation."[7] In particular, stanza 99 describes a leader named Gwawrddur:

> He charged before three hundred of the finest,
> He cut down both center and wing,
> He excelled in the forefront of the noblest host,
> He gave gifts of horses from the herd in winter.
> He fed black ravens on the rampart of a fortress
> Though he was no Arthur.

translation by A.O.H. Jarman [8]

"This passage establishes that by middle of the seventh century at the latest there existed in Britain a conception of a historical figure named Arthur who was so greatly renowned that even a ruler who would charge three hundred men cannot match up to him."[9] "Some scholars take this reference to indicate that a figure called Arthur was so famous at the time of the poem's original composition that a warrior could be praised simply by comparison."[10] Dr. Rachel Bromwich cites passage 99 as support for "her argument that 'the historical Arthur was a north-British leader or chieftain who lived *circa* 500'"[11] We assert that Arthur was here spoken of as a kinsman, a hero of the past horse culture of the Gododdin, so well known that only his name be mentioned without further explanation to represent greatness.

## *Y Goddodin* Notes

[1] Aneirin: *Y Gododdin*, translated by AOH Jarman, 1990. Flyleaf.

[2] ibid

[3] *Y Gododdin*. http://everything2.com/title/Y%2520Gododdin. Retrieved May 18, 2011.

[4] Aneirin: *Y Gododdin*, translated by AOH Jarman, 1990. Introduction page xlii

[5] ibid Introduction pages xliii-xlv

[6] ibid Introduction page xlv

[7] ibid Introduction page xxxiv

[8] *Y Gododdin*. http://everything2.com/title/Y%2520Gododdin. Retrieved May 18, 2011.

[9] ibid

[10] Siân Echard's Medieval and Arthurian Pages. *Y Gododdin*. http://faculty.arts.ubc.ca/sechard/492godo.htm . Retrieved May 18, 2011.

[11] Aneirin: *Y Gododdin*, translated by AOH Jarman, 1990. Notes page 150.

# Map of the

N

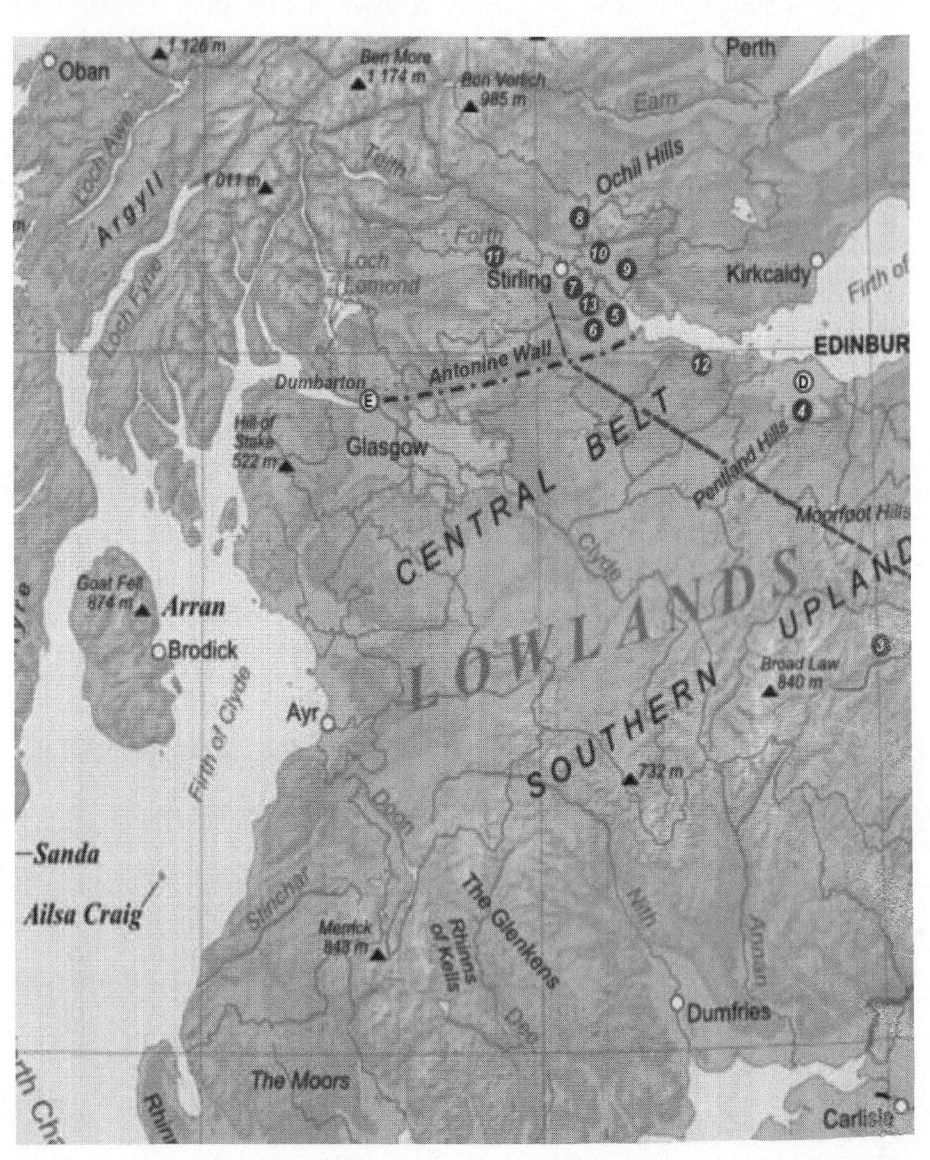
Oban
Ben More
1 174 m
985 m
Perth
Earn
Teith
Ochil Hills
Loch Awe
Argyll
1 011 m
Forth
Loch Lomond
Loch Fyne
Stirling
Kirkcaldy
Firth of
EDINBUR
Antonine Wall
Dumbarton
Glasgow
Hill of Stake
522 m
CENTRAL BELT
Pentland Hills
Moorfoot Hills
Clyde
LOWLANDS
SOUTHERN UPLAND
Goat Fell
874 m
Arran
Brodick
Firth of Clyde
Ayr
Broad Law
840 m
732 m
Doon
Sanda
Ailsa Craig
Stinchar
Merrick
843 m
Rhinns of Kells
The Glenkens
Nith
Annan
Dumfries
Dee
The Moors
Carlisle

# Gododdin Campaign

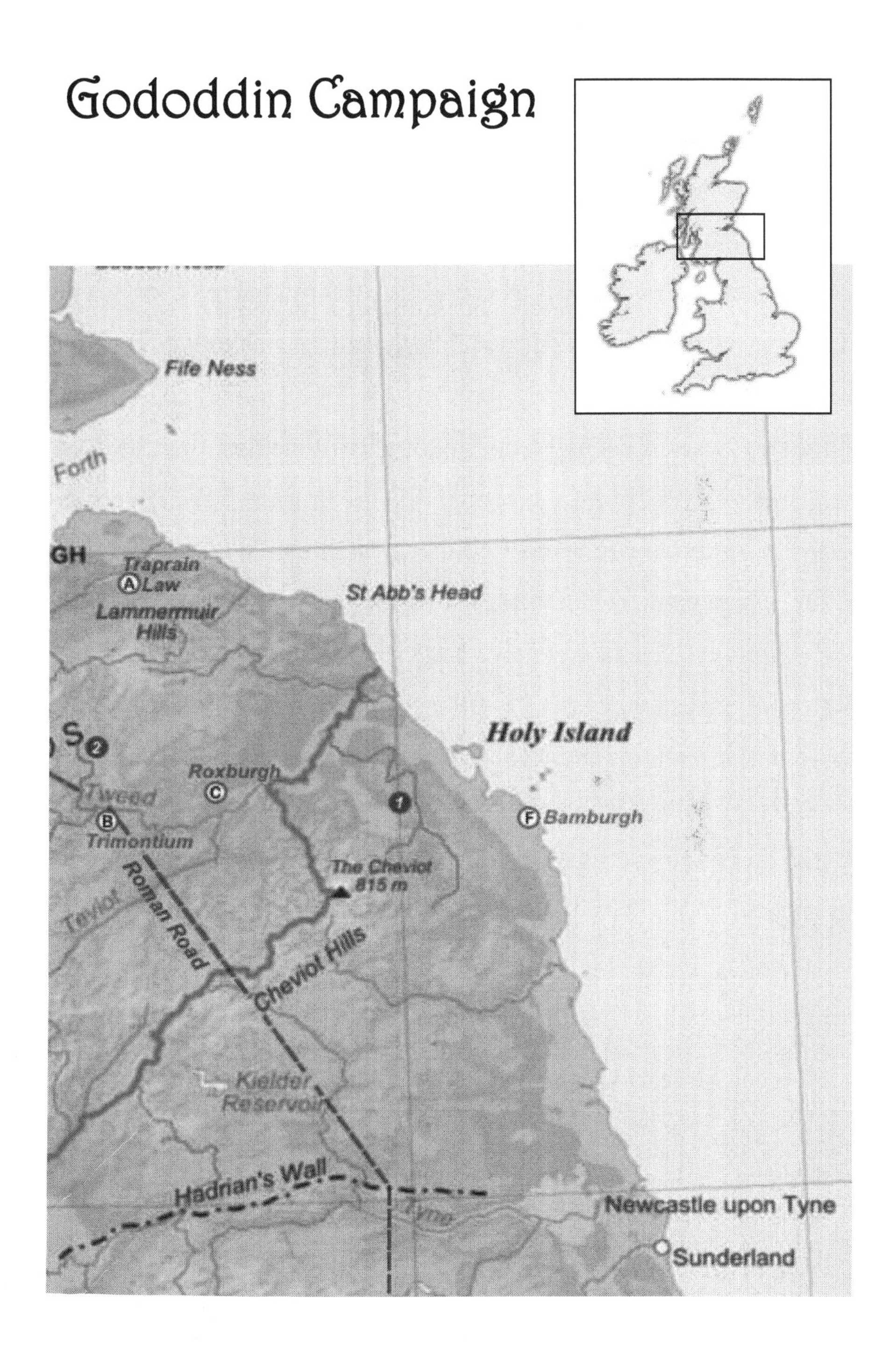

## Map of the Gododdin Campaign

### The Gododdin Campaign to secure the lands of his people

In looking at battle lists suggesting Northern sites, we have combined various texts with geographical information and knowledge of military tactics to offer our own interpretations, making no claim for the final truth but to open the door to discussion and stimulate continuing research. Our suggested order of battles represents six campaign seasons from Yeavering Bell to Bouden Hill, covering a period of approximately eight years. In addition, we have included Arthur's final battle at Camelon.

Nennius described twelve battles at locations not known today. We have interpreted his locations according to place names, geographical features, and local lore. Additionally, we have rearranged the order of battles which Nennius may have listed according to the poetic, rhyming patterns of early oral traditions, into a logical military campaign.

## Map of the Gododdin Campaign

| ● | Arthur's 12 Battles | |
|---|---|---|
| Battle | Name | Year |
| 1 | Yeavering Bell/River Glein | 508 |
| 2 | Stow in Wedale/ fortress of Guinnion | 509 |
| 3 | Yarrow/Cat Coit Celidon | 509 |
| 4 | Edinburgh/Mount Agnet | 510 |
| 5 | Camelon/City of the Legion | 511 |
| 6 | Dunipais/above river called Bassas | 511 |
| 7, 8, 9, 10 | Stirling/above River Dubglas | 512 |
| 11 | Fords of Frew/River Tribruit | 513 |
| 12 | Boudon Hill/Mount Badon | 516 |
| 13 | Camelon/Camlann | 537 |

## Places of Importance

| ○ | Places of Importance |
|---|---|
| A | Traprain Law |
| B | Trimontium & Eildon Hill North |
| C | Roxburgh |
| D | Edinburgh |
| E | Dumbarton/Alcuid |
| F | Bamburgh |

**A Traprain Law**

Ancient capital of the Gododdin. Dome-shaped hill twenty miles east of Edinburgh. Located nearby is the Loth Stone which is believed to mark the grave of King Loth (Lot) for whom the Lothians are named.

**B Trimontium (Eildon Hill North)**

The Roman fort located in the shadow of Eildon Hill North on the border between the Selgovae and Gododdin tribes.

**C Roxburgh**

Known in the time of Arthur as Marchidun, meaning cavalry fort, Roxburgh is positioned between two rivers on a narrow strip of land formed by their confluence. It was occupied and fortified by the Gododdin after the Romans abandoned Trimontium.

**D Edinburgh**

The Gododdin moved their capital to Edinburgh from Traprain Law circa 500.

**E Dumbarton/Alcluid**

Just west of Glasgow, Dumbarton Rock was a stronghold of the Damnonii tribe, one of Arthur's allies.

**F Bamburgh**

Angle mercenary settlement ruled by King Oesa circa 500.

## The Gododdin Campaign

### 1. Year 508: The first battle in which Arthur defeated the Angles at Yeavering Bell.

**"...at the mouth of the river which is called Glein."**

*Nennius Battle 1*

On the frontier of the land of the Gododdin, at the base of Yeavering Bell, runs the River Glen (Glein). Arthur, a young war leader prepared for his first battle with a war band of equestrian-minded friends. He brought his war band to the larger army formed at Roxburgh, from where they marched down to relieve the threat to Yeavering Bell by Oesa's Angles. Arthur was sent ahead to scout for the main army because he was on horseback. He took advantage of the situation, attacked the Angle camp with cavalry, drove them out, and, using mobility, tactics, and the river as an ally, ran them all down as they were moving east on the open ground. Today the Battle Stone stands at Yeavering Bell.

### 2. Year 509: The second battle in which Arthur defeated the Angles at Stow in Wedale.

**"...at the fortress of Guinnion ."**

*Nennius Battle 8*

The Picts crossed the Gala Water into Gododdin lands from their southern outpost at Ring Hill. At Guinnion (white place or holy place) Arthur met them. Defending the Christian site of the chapel of St. Mary at Stow, Arthur used what would become one of his signature tactics. He set the battle with his infantry and then crushed the Angles with his mobile cavalry.

### 3. Year 509: The third battle in which Arthur defeated the Picts at Yarrow in the Wood of Celidon.

**"...in the forest of Celidon, that is Cat Coit Celidon."**

*Nennius Battle 7*

Located in the ancient forest of Cat Coit Celidon is Yarrow where a great battle was fought as evidenced by the discovery of thirteen Christian warrior graves and a battle stone that marks where two Damnonian princes fell. The Gododdin and Damnonii marched there to join their cousins in driving the Picts from Selgovae land, which would also secure the western border of the Gododdin territory. Using flat ground close by a river with fords became another tactic that allowed for maximum effectiveness of his cavalry. The second campaign season ended with Arthur, victorious in two more battles, returning to winter at Roxburgh.

### 4. Year 510: The fourth battle in which Arthur defeated the Picts at Edinburgh.

**"...on the mountain which is called Agnet."**

*Nennius Battle 11*

A large community was centered around a Pict broch atop the rock at Agnet (Edinburgh) located west of the Gododdin capital of Traprain Law. Arthur moved against them to eliminate the nearby threat to his capital. Using the crags above Edinburgh (Arthur's Seat) to plan his attack, and viewing the early stages of the battle from that elevated vantage point, he moved his cavalry down to exploit the weaknesses in the Pict battle line north of the old Roman fort. Their military arm scattered in the battle, the Pict population abandoned Edinburgh rock.

In the fall of that year, King Lot moved the Gododdin capital from Traprain Law to Edinburgh. With this victory, Arthur was recognized by the King as the warlord of the Gododdin.

**5. Year 511: The fifth battle in which Arthur defeated the Picts at Camelon.**

**"...in the City of the Legion."**

*Nennius Battle 9*

This would be the first battle in a momentus endeavor to reconquer the Manau-Gododdin, the first battle of which would be at Camelon (City of the Legion). Arthur's cavalry swept in to surprise the Picts and cut them off from supplies and reinforcements via the ford at the old Roman bridge. After a short siege, the unprepared Pictish garrison gave up the run-down Roman fort, fleeing to the west. Arthur now held the location that would be his headquarters and home for many years to come.

**6. Year 511: The sixth battle in which Arthur defeated the Picts at Dunipais.**

**"...above the river which is called Bassas."**

*Nennius Battle 6*

The Picts reorganized their southern border and assembled an army at the twin mounds or Bassas near Dunipais at the junction of the Carron River and the River Bonney. Arthur did not block the ford at the old Roman bridge this time. He allowed half the Pict army to cross, then deployed his infantry to cause a bottleneck at the ford. Sweeping in with his cavalry around the flank of his infantry, he crushed the Picts on the south bank. By cutting the head off the snake, the other disorganized half of the Pict force did not choose to advance.

### 7. Year 512: The seventh, eighth, ninth, and tenth battles in which Arthur defeated the Picts near Stirling. "...above another river which is called Dubglas and is in the region of Linnuis."

*Nennius Battles 2, 3, 4, 5*

Assuming the Dubglas (dark river in P-Celtic) is the peat-colored River Forth at Stirling, it well falls within the region of Linnuis (meaning firth in Q-Celtic). Around the River Forth and Stirling, Arthur fought a victorious campaign of four battles.

The seventh battle secured the Stirling hill fort south of the River Forth. Arthur's infantry held the Pict garrison in the fort, while Arthur and his cavalry denied Pict reinforcements from crossing the ford. The Picts surrendered the Stirling fort.

### 8. Year 512: The seventh, eighth, ninth, and tenth battles in which Arthur defeated the Picts near Stirling. "...above another river which is called Dubglas

**and is in the region of Linnuis.”**

*Nennius Battles 2, 3, 4, 5*

Assuming the Dubglas (dark river in P-Celtic) is the peat-colored River Forth at Stirling, it well falls within the region of Linnuis (meaning firth in Q-Celtic). Around the River Forth and Stirling, Arthur fought a victorious campaign of four battles.

The eighth battle was fought across the River Forth and up the Allen Water valley. There the Picts were organizing a force to retake Stirling. Arthur moved quickly to attack and disperse them before they could mount their offensive.

**9. Year 512: The seventh, eighth, ninth, and tenth battles in which Arthur defeated the Picts near Stirling.**

**“...above another river which is called Dubglas**

**and is in the region of Linnuis.”**

*Nennius Battles 2, 3, 4, 5*

Assuming the Dubglas (dark river in P-Celtic) is the peat-colored River Forth at Stirling, it well falls within the region of Linnuis (meaning firth in Q-Celtic). Around the River Forth and Stirling, Arthur fought a victorious campaign of four battles.

In the ninth battle, Arthur moved east along the north bank of the River Forth and engaged the Picts at Clackmannan. Using ground that was perfect for his army, Arthur drove the Picts east out of what had been Manau-Gododdin land.

## 10. Year 512: The seventh, eighth, ninth, and tenth battles in which Arthur defeated the Picts near Stirling.

**"...above another river which is called Dubglas and is in the region of Linnuis."**

*Nennius Battles 2, 3, 4, 5*

Assuming the Dubglas (dark river in P-Celtic) is the peat-colored River Forth at Stirling, it well falls within the region of Linnuis (meaning firth in Q-Celtic). Around the River Forth and Stirling, Arthur fought a victorious campaign of four battles.

In the tenth battle, the Picts attacked down from Dumyat in the Ochil Hills toward Stirling. This attack was heroic but hastily launched. Arthur reacted quickly and defeated them on a flat-topped hill near the Airthrey Stone, close to where the Wallace Monument stands today. After four defeats in a row, the Picts of the region were spent.

## 11. Year 513: The eleventh battle in which Arthur defeated the Picts at the Fords of Frew.

**"...on the banks of a river which is called Tribruit."**

*Nennius Battle 10*

Three (tri) rushing rivers (bruit), the River Forth, the Goodie Water, and the River Teith, come together in the Vale of Menteith west of Stirling. In a final attempt to win back Sitrling, a western Pictish army moved to the only other strategic crossing point of the River Forth, the Fords of Frew. Arthur's army marched west along the south bank of the Forth and met them. Attacking and defeating half the

Pict force after it crossed, Arthur fell back to regroup, thinking the Picts would withdraw. However, they pressed the attack with the other half of their army and total defeat was the outcome. The Picts withdrew well up the river Teith valley to their hill forts.

**12. Year 516: the twelfth battle in which Arthur defeated the Saxons at Bouden Hill.**

**"...on Mount Badon."**

*Nennius Battle 12*

The Battle of Bouden Hill (Mount Badon) was fought hard by the River Avon west of Edinburgh near Linlithgow. Arthur's cavalry-only force discovered the landing of a huge Saxon raiding party, perhaps 1000 warriors, at the mouth of the Avon. Arthur tried to fight them at first with only the cavalry he had at hand, but was forced to withdraw to the safety of Bouden Hill. Beseiged there for three days, Arthur waited until Gododdini infantry arrived from Camelon and Edinburgh. Fearing encirclement, the Saxons moved toward their boats, finding themselves fighting their way through a gauntlet of Gododdin flank attacks. Arthur's cavalry then charged down from Bouden Hill and eliminated the Saxons piecemeal at the ford and at the beach. One thousand Saxons lay dead. This is the battle that ensured peace for the Gododdin for a generation.

# The Final Battle

## Year 537: the final battle in which Arthur fell to the Picts and Saxons at Camelon.

**"The battle of Camlann in which Arthur and Medraut perished"**

*Annales Cambriae*

Arthur must ride out to defend his people once more. Twenty-one years after Bouden Hill, a combined Pict/Saxon force moved against Camelon. Arthur and his remaining followers are older, but they will not die easy. Arthur deployed against this enemy north of the crook in the River Carron. Some young warriors rode with him, most notably Medraut, who was at his side. In a battle that pitted a fierce foot army against veteran heavy cavalry, both sides were decimated. Arthur and Medraut fell fighting back to back and were carried from the field by the few survivors of Arthur's war band. Monks recorded that at the Battle of Camlann (Camelon) both "Arthur and Medraut fell: and there was plague in Britain and Ireland."[1]

[1] Medieval Sourcebook: Nennius: *Historia Brittonum*, 8th century. Chapter 56 Lupack, Alan (Trans.) for The Camelot Project.
http://www.fordham.edu/halsall/basis/nennius-full.html Retrieved November 7, 2010.
http://www.fordham.edu/halsall/source/annalescambriae.html Retrieved November 7, 2010.

*Arthur of the Gododdin*

## Selected Sources

Alain de Lille. Commentary on *Prophetia Anglicana.* Frankfort, 1603.

*Annales Cambriae.* (c956). In *Internet Medieval Sourcebook.* [http://www.fordham.edu/halsall/sbook.html]. March 2009.

Day, D. (1995). *The Search for King Arthur.* New York: Facts on File, Inc.

Evans, J.G. (ed.). (1906). *Black Book of Carmarthen.* Pwllheli.

Fletcher, R.H. (1906). *The Arthurian Material in the Chronicles.* 2nd edition by Roger Sherman Loomis, New York: Burt Franklin 1973.

Gildas. (c546). *De Excidio Britanniae.* In *Internet Medieval Sourcebook.* [http://www.fordham.edu/halsall/sbook.html]. March 2009.

Glennie, J.S.S. (1869/2003). *Arthurian Localities.* Edinburgh: Edmonston and Douglas. Whitefish, MT: Kessinger Publishing.

Goodrich, N.L. (1986). *King Arthur.* New York: Harper & Row.

Green, T. (2004). *The Monstrous Regiment of Arthurs.* [http://www.arthuriana.co.uk/historicity/arthurappendix.htm]. March 2009.

Jarman, A.O.H. (ed. and trans.). (1988). *Aneirn: Y Gododdin.* Llandysul, Dyfed: The Gomer Press.

Lambert de St. Omer. (1120). *Libre Floridus.*

McHardy, S. (2001). *The Quest for Arthur.* Edinburgh: Luath Press.

Moffat, A. (1999). *Arthur and the Lost Kingdoms.* London: Weidenfeld & Nicolson.

Morris, J. (1973). *The Age of Arthur.* New York: Charles Scribner's Sons.

Nennius. (c810). *Historia Britonum.* In *Internet Medieval Sourcebook.* [http://www.fordham.edu/halsall/sbook.html]. March 2009.

Pryor, F. (Narrator). (2004). *King Arthur's Britain* [DVD]. Silver Springs, MD: Acorn Media (Channel Four International Limited).

Russell, J.E. (2005). *The Historical Arthur of Galloway.* [http://www.gatehouse-of-fleet.co.uk/arthurofgalloway.htm].

Skene, W.F. (1988). *Arthur and the Britons in Wales and Scotland.* Edinburgh: Llanerch Enterprises.

Snyder, C. (2000). *The World of King Arthur.* London: Thames & Hudson Ltd.

White, R (ed.) (1997). *King Arthur in Legend and History.* London: J.M. Dent.

## About the Authors

### Michael A. Ferenz

"King Arthur. My first experience with him was as a young boy of five. My father read to me from a scrapbook of comic strip clippings "A Story of Prince Valiant" who had come to the court of King Arthur. Much later while serving in the army and stationed in Germany, I traveled to Innsbruck, Austria, and visited the Hofkirche, the tomb of Maximilian I, Holy Roman Emperor. The tourist brochure described Maximilian's sarcophagus as being surrounded by larger than life bronze statues of his "relatives and contemporaries." Surprised and puzzled I was when I came upon the statue of King Arthur. I thought, "He is not a real person. What is he doing here?""

Some time after visiting the tomb, Michael read Geoffrey Ashe's Arthurian theory which left him with a lot of questions, particularly Ashe's suggested time line. He didn't pursue it at that time, but later, on finding Norma Lorre Goodrich's book *King Arthur*, he thought she brought together linguistics, geography, history, and chronology in a way that shed new light on the ancient legend.

In creating the story *Arthur of the Gododdin*, Michael used his military experience and knowledge of tactics, history, and topography to plan an organized campaign consistent with the tribal culture of Arthur's time. Research led Michael to contemporary authors Stuart McHardy, Alistair Moffat, and J. E. Russell, among others, and ancient sources such as the poem *Y Goddodin*, the *Historia Brittonum* of Nennius, and the *Annales Cambriae.* Imagining what it would have been like to see the great Arthur riding into Edinburgh victorious after the battle of Mt. Badon, inspired Michael to plant the seeds of historical truths within a fictional first-person, eyewitness account set in the sixth century.

**Christine J. Brookes**

"Arthur called to me from the shelves of a used bookstore in San Antonio, Texas, in the early 1990s. I had been browsing the shelves for a good read for the plane flight home. Seeing nothing of interest, I started out the back door, glancing at the last rows of shelves. In bold letters against the green spine of a paperback, I read KING ARTHUR. In Norma Lorre Goodrich's first paragraph, she states her intentions "to offer the first historical proof of the existence of King Arthur. (p. 3) I was hooked."

As a literature teacher, Chris knows there is a kernel of truth behind every legend. A truth that may have been known so long ago there is no proof of it today. Goodrich's claim to offer proof intrigued and inspired her to go beyond the legends she had been teaching to seventh graders. In the last twenty years since the publication of Goodrich's book, many others have published research and theories on the subject of the historicity of Arthur. Books today generally assume the reality of an historical Arthur, but authors are still divided on the question of the location of Arthur's origin.

In the midst of planning to follow Arthur's footsteps through England, Chris was reminded of Goodrich's words, "It is also possible to suggest that the historical Arthur fought most of his battles in northern Britain, and that his association with Wales, Glastonbury, and other southern locations came much later." (Goodrich p. xxx) Turning her steps north to Scotland, she, surprisingly, discovered that the Scots, in general, treated questions about Arthur with indifference. He has apparently been so transformed by English writers and accepted as a model for English kings, many Scots have given up all claim on him.

Chris, however, believes in Arthur as a Man of the North and continues to explore Arthurian locations and pursue Arthurian connections in Scotland. Recently 'The Inheritance of Arthur,' a conference held in Edinburgh, surveyed the current state of knowledge on Arthur and his cultural context, and encouraged people across Scotland to re-evaluate and reclaim their place in the Arthurian tradition. Chris's collaboration with Michael Ferenz is an opportunity to present, in historical fiction, the Northern Theory in a plausible context.

Printed in Great Britain
by Amazon.co.uk, Ltd.,
Marston Gate.